On Your Mark,
Get Set, Laugh!

by Nancy Krulik • illustrated by John & Wendy

Grosset & Dunlap

D0503262

For Lauren and Alexandra, who
are headed down the right track!—N.K.

For Don—a real good sport!—J&W

The scanning, uploading, and distribution of this book via the Internet or
via any other means without the permission of the publisher is illegal and
punishable by law. Please purchase only authorized electronic editions,
and do not participate in or encourage electronic piracy of copyrighted
materials. Your support of the author's rights is appreciated.

Text copyright © 2004 by Nancy Krulik. Illustrations copyright © 2004 by
John and Wendy. All rights reserved. Published by Grosset & Dunlap, a
division of Penguin Young Readers Group, 345 Hudson Street, New York,
New York 10014. GROSSET & DUNLAP is a trademark of Penguin Group
(USA) Inc. Printed in the U.S.A.

Library of Congress Cataloging-in-Publication Data

Krulik, Nancy E.
   On your mark, get set, laugh! / by Nancy Krulik ; illustrated by John &
Wendy.
      p. cm. — (Katie Kazoo, switcheroo ; 13)
   Summary: When fourth-grade Katie turns into her unfair track coach, she
gives all the kids on the team a chance to compete, including the slowest
runner in her class.
   ISBN 0-448-43605-1 (pbk.)
   [1. Track and field—Fiction. 2. Schools—Fiction. 3. Teamwork (Sports)—
Fiction. 4. Magic—Fiction.] I. John & Wendy. II. Title.

PZ7.K9416On 2004
   [Fic]—dc22   2004005226

            ISBN 0-448-43605-1   10 9 8 7

Chapter 1

"I . . . can't . . . run . . . much . . . more," Katie Carew huffed and puffed as she ran beside her friend Emma Weber.

"Me neither," Emma said, gasping for air. "This seems a lot longer than a mile!"

Katie agreed. Her legs felt like limp spaghetti. And she still had another lap to go.

Gym class sure had changed from last year. When Katie was in third grade, gym had been so much fun. The gym teacher let the kids play fun games like Steal the Bacon and Crab Soccer.

But now that she was a fourth-grader, things were different. For starters, gym wasn't called *gym* anymore. The new gym teacher, Coach Debbie, called it *physical education.*

Coach Debbie was tough on the fourth-graders. She wanted them all to be able to run a mile in ten minutes or less by the end of the year.

Mandy Banks and Andrew Epstein were *really* fast runners. They could already run a ten-minute mile. Emma Stavros, Kadeem Carter, and Kevin Camilleri had all almost made it.

Katie wasn't so fast. She and Emma W. were usually pretty far behind the rest of the class. But at least Katie wasn't last.

George Brennan always held that spot. He was the slowest runner in class 4A.

"Not bad, girls!" Coach Debbie told Katie and Emma as they crossed the finish line. She clicked her stopwatch. "You did that in fourteen minutes."

"That's a full minute faster than last time," Katie said, out of breath.

"But it's still not a ten-minute mile," Emma W. said. She bent over and rested her hands on her knees.

"Walk it off, girls," Coach Debbie told Katie and Emma. "We've got to wait for George to pull up the rear anyhow."

Katie looked out on the track. George sure seemed tired. He wasn't running anymore. He was walking the last lap.

"George needs to get new sneakers," Kadeem told the kids.

"Why?" Emma S. asked.

"Because right now he's just a *loafer*!" Kadeem chuckled at his own joke.

Katie didn't laugh. "Nobody can be good at everything," Katie reminded Kadeem.

"Yeah, but George isn't good at *anything*," Kadeem insisted.

"He is too!" Kevin leaped up to defend his best friend. "George is the funniest kid in the whole fourth grade. He would never have told a lame joke like that shoe one you just told."

Kadeem frowned. Katie knew that Kadeem thought he was the funniest kid in the fourth grade.

When George finally crossed the finish line, Coach Debbie clicked her stopwatch. "Eighteen minutes, George. Same as yesterday."

"At least I didn't do worse," he said.

"We'll get you in shape yet," Coach Debbie assured him.

George thought for a moment. "I guess I would do better if I had a cold."

"Why's that?" Coach Debbie asked.

"Because I'd have a racing pulse and a running nose!" He laughed really hard. So did everyone else in the class.

"See, I told you," Kevin told Kadeem. "George is the funniest kid in the fourth grade!"

Coach Debbie shook her head sternly. "Physical fitness is no laughing matter," she reminded the boys.

George and Kevin bit their lips to keep from giggling.

"Anyway, I have an exciting announcement!" Coach Debbie exclaimed. "It's track team season! Since you're in fourth grade now, you kids can be on the team. Fourth, fifth, and sixth-graders can join."

The kids all started talking at once. They were really excited.

"I have to warn you," the coach continued. "The kids on *my* track team will have to work hard! You've got to be physically fit if you want to beat the other schools."

"When are the tryouts?" Mandy asked.

The smile fell from Coach Debbie's face. "Cherrydale Elementary School does not allow tryouts for sports teams. Anyone who wants to can be on the team. That's Principal Kane's rule." She sighed and shook her head. "I have no choice but to do what the principal tells me to."

Katie was confused. Principal Kane's rule meant everyone had a chance to play for their school. But Coach Debbie did not seem happy about that. In fact, she seemed kind of angry. That was strange. Usually, teachers *wanted* kids to volunteer for things.

Obviously, Coach Debbie wasn't a usual kind of teacher.

Chapter 2

When physical education was over, Katie walked back to her classroom with the rest of the kids. She was still pretty tired from all that running. She and Emma were the last ones in the door of room 4A.

"Check out Mr. Guthrie!" George shouted. "He looks like Abraham Lincoln."

Katie looked at her teacher. He was wearing a fake beard, a black jacket, and a stovepipe hat. Katie poked Emma in the ribs and laughed. Emma giggled at their teacher too.

Mr. Guthrie was always doing things like that. Just last week, Mr. Guthrie had dressed like King Tut for math class. He'd made the class build pyramids out of plastic bricks. Piling those bricks up just right was harder than Katie had thought.

Mr. Guthrie wasn't like any teacher Katie had ever had before. Especially not Mrs. Derkman!

Last year, in third grade, Katie's teacher had been Mrs. Derkman, the strictest teacher in the whole school. She had lots of rules in her classroom. The desks in her room were all in neat rows. And the kids had to sit in their assigned seats all year long.

That wasn't the way things were in Mr. Guthrie's class. For starters, there weren't any desks in class 4A. The kids sat in beanbag chairs and leaned on clipboards to do their written work.

Mr. Guthrie let the kids decorate their own beanbag chairs. During the first month of school, when they were studying birds, they'd turned their beanbags into nests.

Now, they were about to begin a history

project. So Mr. Guthrie had asked the kids to decorate their beanbag chairs to represent important periods in American history.

Katie was really proud of her design. Her beanbag looked like the first American flag. She'd glued a circle of thirteen white paper stars to her beanbag, and added red and white streamers to make stripes.

Emma W.'s beanbag was right next to Katie's. She'd built a cardboard model of the Statue of Liberty on her seat. Katie thought it looked amazing!

"I hope we get to be partners for the history project," Emma whispered to Katie as they sat down on their beanbags.

Katie nodded. "I hope so too."

Last year, Katie would have wanted either Jeremy Fox or Suzanne Lock for her partner. They were Katie's best friends in the whole world. But they weren't in Katie's class this year. They were in class 4B with Ms. Sweet.

At first, Katie had been sad that she wasn't in a class with her best friends. But it hadn't turned out so bad. Katie still played with Jeremy and Suzanne after school. And Katie and Emma had become really good friends, too.

"Check out George," Kevin told the class. He pointed toward George's beanbag.

George had decorated his seat to look like the rowboat George Washington had used during the Revolutionary War.

"Stroke! Stroke!" George called out. He was standing on his beanbag, pretending to be George Washington. "Hey, do you guys know why pictures of George Washington always show him standing?"

"Why?" Katie wondered.

"Because he would *never* lie!"

Everyone started to laugh . . . except Kadeem. He opened his mouth to tell a joke of his own.

But Mr. Guthrie stopped him. "Not now, dude," the teacher told Kadeem. "Save it. I'll let you guys have a joke-off later today."

Katie smiled. She loved George and Kadeem's joke-offs. They told their best jokes, and then Mr. Guthrie let the class vote on who was funnier. George had won the last joke-off, so Katie was pretty sure

Kadeem would have some great jokes today.

But for now, it was time to get to work.

"Okay, you guys, here comes the moment you've been waiting for!" Mr. Guthrie announced. "I'm going to assign history partners. You have to work together to come up with a topic. Then you have to plan and present an oral report."

Emma looked over at Katie and crossed her fingers.

Katie crossed her fingers too. Then she held her breath and waited.

Chapter 3

"Okay," Mr. Guthrie began, "Mandy, you and George will be working together.

"Andrew, you and Emma . . ."

Oh, no! Katie gasped.

". . . Stavros," Mr. Guthrie continued, "are partners."

Phew. Wrong Emma.

"Now, Katie Kazoo, it's time for you," Mr. Guthrie teased, using the super-cool nickname George had given her. "You and Kadeem will be paired up for this one."

This is horrible, Katie thought to herself. *I wish . . .*

Katie was about to say that she wished she could have any other partner besides Kadeem.

But she stopped herself. Katie didn't make wishes anymore. She knew what could happen when they came true.

It had all started one day at the beginning of third grade. Katie had lost the football game for her team, ruined her favorite pair of pants, and let out a big burp in front of the whole class. That night, Katie had wished she could be anyone but herself.

There must have been a shooting star overhead when she made that wish, because the very next day, the magic wind came.

The magic wind was a wild tornado that blew just around Katie. It was so powerful that every time it came, it turned her into somebody else! Katie never knew when the wind would arrive. But whenever it did, her whole world was turned upside down . . . *switcheroo*!

The first time the magic wind came, it had turned Katie into Speedy, class 3A's hamster! That morning, Katie had escaped from the hamster cage and wound up stuck inside

George's stinky sneaker! Luckily, Katie had switched back into herself before George could step on her.

The magic wind came back again and again after that. Sometimes, it changed Katie into other kids—like Jeremy, Emma, and Suzanne's baby sister, Heather. One time, it even turned her into Mrs. Derkman. Katie had almost had to kiss the teacher's husband, Freddy. *That would have been so gross!*

Katie never knew when the magic wind would return. All she knew was that when it did, she was going to wind up getting into some sort of trouble.

That's why Katie didn't make wishes anymore. She didn't want them to come true.

The way Katie figured it, with Kadeem as her partner, she didn't need any more problems.

Chapter 4

At three o'clock on Thursday, Katie and Emma raced out onto the field behind the school. They were very excited. Today was the first track team practice.

The fifth and sixth-graders were huddled together near a tree. Some of them were stretching their legs, getting ready to run.

Mandy, Jeremy, Kevin, and Andrew were practicing their long jumps. After each jump, they measured who had gone the farthest.

Katie and Emma walked over to where the fourth-graders were jumping.

"Hey, you guys," Jeremy greeted them. "Isn't this cool?"

Katie nodded, but didn't say anything. She was a little nervous.

"You know, last year the track team went for ice cream every time they won a meet," he continued.

Emma smiled. "Then I hope we win *every* meet," she said. "I can't get enough chocolate, chocolate chip!"

"I like cookie dough," Jeremy told her.

Just then, Suzanne came racing up to them. "Hi, guys!" She was wearing navy running pants and a matching sweat jacket. She looked like a real track star.

"I didn't know you liked running track," Jeremy said to her. "I thought all you cared about was that modeling class you take on Wednesdays."

"Running's okay," Suzanne admitted. "But I'm *really* here to hang out with fifth and sixth-graders! They hardly ever talk to us. So this is my chance."

Jeremy looked over to where the older kids were stretching. It didn't seem like they even noticed that the fourth-graders were there!

"They're *still* not talking to us," Jeremy told Suzanne.

"They will," Suzanne assured him. "They have to. *We're a team.* Look, here comes the coach now."

"Hello, track team!" Coach Debbie greeted them. "Are we ready for a winning season?"

"Yeah!" the kids shouted back.

"I can't hear you!" Coach Debbie said.

"Yeah!" The kids screamed louder.

"Great!" the coach said. "Because today,

you're going to work harder than you ever have before. You're going to discover muscles you never knew you had. It's going to be tough. But it's worth it. After all, you are the few, the proud, the Track Team!"

Katie gulped. Coach Debbie sounded more like a general in the army than a teacher.

"You have to be physically fit to win track meets. You've got to be ready for anything!" Coach Debbie continued. "Track meets are full of surprises."

At that moment, the team's *first* surprise arrived.

"Sorry I'm late!" George huffed as he ran onto the field. "It took me a while to tie my new sneakers." He held out his foot to show off his new running shoes.

Coach Debbie seemed more shocked than anyone to see George there. "*You're* joining the track team?" she asked him. She did not sound happy.

George nodded. "Sure. My dad was on the

track team when he was in high school. He
thought it was fun."

Coach Debbie turned red in the face.
"*Fun*? Track is not about fun! Track is about
winning! We are here to WIN! WIN! WIN! If
it weren't about winning, they wouldn't bother
to keep score."

George gulped. "Sorry," he said.

"You're going to be," Coach Debbie assured him. "Now drop and give me ten."

"Ten what?" George asked.

"I think she means push-ups," Katie told him.

"Exactly," Coach Debbie agreed.

Katie smiled proudly.

"And since you're so smart," Coach Debbie continued, "you can give me ten, too. In fact, everyone can. That's what happens on my team when someone arrives late to practice."

She lifted her silver whistle to her lips and blew . . . hard. "Okay, enough chitchat. One . . . two . . ."

"George, this is all your fault!" Suzanne said as she did her push-ups.

"Yeah, thanks a lot," Mandy added.

George's face turned red. Katie couldn't tell if he was embarrassed, or just having a hard time doing push-ups.

One thing was for sure, though. The track team wasn't nearly as much fun as she'd thought it would be.

Chapter 5

On Friday morning, Katie was in pain. Every one of her muscles was stiff because of yesterday's tough track practice. She was not in a good mood at all.

And working with Kadeem on the history project was just making things worse.

"Here's a good topic," Katie suggested. The class was in the library doing research for their projects. She pointed to a chapter in one of the history books. "We can do our report on the first Thanksgiving. We could dress as Pilgrims and . . ."

"Do you know what kind of music the Pilgrims danced to?" Kadeem asked her.

Katie looked in the book. It didn't say anything about music. "No. What kind?"

"Plymouth *rock*!" Kadeem chuckled.

Katie laughed—a little. It was a funny joke after all. But there really wasn't time for fun. They had too much work to do. She stood up to get another book.

"Hey, where are you going?" Kadeem asked.

"To get another history book. We have to pick a topic."

"Speaking of picking," Kadeem said, "did you ever hear this one? You can pick your friends, you can pick your nose, but you should never, *ever* pick your friend's nose!" Then he picked up a paper airplane and threw it across the room.

That was gross! Katie had had enough of Kadeem. So instead of getting a new history book, she decided to walk over to Mr. Guthrie.

"Hey, Katie," he greeted her. "How's it going?"

"Terrible," Katie moaned.

"Anything I can do to help?" Mr. Guthrie asked.

"You can give me another partner for this project," Katie suggested hopefully.

"Sorry, kiddo. No can do," he replied. "Everyone's all paired up."

"Then I can work by myself," Katie volunteered. She looked over at Kadeem. "I'm sort of doing that anyhow."

Mr. Guthrie leaned back in his chair. "You're having a hard time working with Kadeem, huh?"

"He's not working at all!" Katie cried out. "I can't get him to agree to any topic. I tried lots of ideas, like the Revolutionary War, the first Thanksgiving, even a biography of Abraham Lincoln. Nothing interests him."

"Oh, something must interest him, Katie," Mr. Guthrie said gently. "Everyone has interests."

"Not Kadeem."

Mr. Guthrie laughed. "Sure he does. And if

you think hard enough, I'm sure you'll figure out what they are."

Katie sighed. Teachers were always doing things like that. They would tell you that the answer was easy. All you had to do was look for it. But they would never tell you what that answer was.

"History isn't just wars, presidents, and important events," Mr. Guthrie continued. "Sometimes, it's told through the lives of ordinary people and the things they liked to do."

"Huh?"

Mr. Guthrie smiled. "You'll make it work. I know you will. There's nothing Katie Kazoo can't do!"

Katie looked back toward Kadeem. Instead of reading a history book, her partner was busy tying his own shoelaces together.

She wasn't so sure.

Chapter 6

After school, Katie and some of her pals went to practice running in Katie's backyard. They wanted to be ready for the big track meet next week.

"Coach Debbie said that on Monday, she'll let us know what races we'll be in," Jeremy told the others. "She's going to post a note on the bulletin board outside the gym."

"I hope I'm in the relay race," Emma said. "I think it's better to be part of a group. That way, if I'm slow, someone else who's fast can help our team catch up."

"I want to jump over the hurdles," Suzanne added. "I've got the perfect legs for it—long,

thin, and muscular."

"I can jump over hurdles too," George said. He leaped up into the air, and spread his legs too.

THUD! George landed right on his rear end. "Ow, my aching butt!" he moaned.

The kids all started giggling. George laughed right along with them. That was George—he would do anything for a laugh.

But at least he knows when to be serious,

Katie thought to herself. *Not like Kadeem.*

"Maybe we should run a few laps," Jeremy suggested.

Katie nodded. "Everybody ready?" she asked.

Suzanne held out her foot so everyone could see her red-and-white running shoe. "My new sneakers are ready to go!"

"So are mine," George said. He held out his foot too. "My dad got me these. They're supposed to make you run like the wind."

"Cool," Jeremy told them. "Then let's run."

Jeremy took the lead, running quickly in circles around Katie's yard. Suzanne, Emma, and Katie all followed behind him.

As usual, George was the slowest of anyone. But Katie could tell he was really trying.

BOOM! Just then, George fell . . . again. *This* time, he landed right on his belly.

"Oops," he groaned as he picked himself up. "I tripped over my new shoelace."

"You ran more like a rock than the wind," Suzanne teased him.

"I don't know why I joined the stupid track team," he said. "I stink."

"No, you don't," Katie tried to tell him.

"Well . . ." Suzanne began to disagree, but the look in Katie's eyes made her stop.

Just then, Pepper, Katie's chocolate-and-white cocker spaniel, ran over to George. *Slurp.* He licked him right on the mouth.

"Blech!" George said, wiping the dog spit from his lips. "What did he do that for?"

"It's his way of telling you that you can do it," Katie told him.

"You can't give up," Emma added.

George didn't seem so sure. "I'm a lousy runner," he told them. "I always get tired before I can finish."

"Maybe you're better at running *short* distances," Jeremy suggested. He pointed to the pine tree across the yard. "Let's see how fast you can run from here to that tree. I'll set my stopwatch."

"Okay," George said.

"On your mark," Jeremy called out. "Get set. Go!"

George ran as fast as he could.

"Ruff! Ruff!" Pepper took off after him. He reached the tree *way* before George did.

"Oh, man," George complained. "Even Katie's dog can beat me."

"He's got four legs instead of two," Katie reminded George. "That makes him twice as fast."

"Maybe we should get Pepper to join the track team," Jeremy joked. "He could be our secret weapon."

"Well, Coach Debbie *did* say that anyone who wanted to could be on the team," George agreed.

"I think you have to be a student at the school, though," Emma said.

George shrugged. "We'll dress him in little doggie jeans and put a hat on his head. Mr. Guthrie will never know he's a dog."

Katie laughed at the thought of Pepper sitting in her classroom, barking out answers to Mr. Guthrie's questions. "George, you crack me up," she told him.

"Wait until you see me in a race," George told her. "I'll really make you laugh then." He started to run again. This time, he made his legs look all wobbly and goofy.

Katie laughed even harder. So did Emma, Suzanne, and Jeremy.

"I hope Coach Debbie has as good of a sense of humor as we do," Suzanne whispered to Katie.

Katie frowned. Somehow, she didn't think so.

Chapter 7

On Monday morning, Katie went with her class to the school library. They were supposed to work on their history projects. Everyone was excited to find information on their topics.

Everyone but Katie and Kadeem, that is. They didn't even *have* a topic yet.

Katie went to the history section of the library and pulled a few books off the shelves. "Here," she said, passing two books to Kadeem. "You look through those, and I'll look at these."

Kadeem opened the cover of one of the books. Then he yawned and closed it again. "This stuff is boring," he said.

"You think the Civil War is boring?"

"It is to me."

Katie sighed. "Well, then how about the California Gold Rush?"

"What's that?" Kadeem asked.

Katie slid a book over to him. "Here, read about it."

"Why don't you just *tell* me?"

But Katie was tired of doing all the work. "Read it," she demanded. "Stop being lazy!"

"I don't feel like it," he told her.

"You don't feel like doing *anything*!" Katie said, banging her fist on the table. "What's wrong with you?"

All the kids stared at Katie.

"Keep your voice down, please," the library teacher said.

Katie hadn't meant to be loud. It was just that she was so frustrated with Kadeem!

Kadeem looked angrily at Katie. "I'm out of here!" He got up and raced out of the library.

Katie followed Kadeem out of the library.

"Go away," Kadeem said, once they were alone in the hallway.

"I'm sorry," Katie told him. "I didn't mean to upset you. I just wanted *you* to read the book for a change."

"Yeah, well, that book's really hard," Kadeem blurted out.

"It's not that hard . . ." Katie began. Then she stopped. "Oh my goodness. Can you read, Kadeem?"

"*Of course* I can read," Kadeem said proudly. Then he frowned. "Just not that well."

"Oh."

"Hey, it's not like I'm stupid or anything," he assured Katie. "I have a learning disability. It makes it hard for me to read. But I'm working with a tutor. I'm getting much better."

"That's good," Katie replied. Now she felt awful for yelling at Kadeem.

"Doing research in books takes me a really

long time," he continued. "I wish I could listen to a tape or watch a video instead. I remember *everything* I hear. One time, I watched this TV show with stand-up comics. I memorized every joke they told."

"Wow!" Katie exclaimed.

Kadeem frowned. "But that doesn't help us."

Katie thought for a moment. Suddenly, she got one of her great ideas. "Maybe it does," she said slowly.

"Huh?"

"I think I've got a great topic for us! But we're going to have to get some help from Mr. Guthrie." She grabbed Kadeem by the hand. "Come on. This is going to be so much fun!"

Chapter 8

Katie was in a great mood after the library. She ran out to the playground for recess.

"Hi, Suzanne!" Katie shouted to her best friend.

"Katie, isn't it awful?" Suzanne said with a frown.

"What?"

"About the track meet," Suzanne told her. "Didn't you see the note Coach Debbie posted?"

Oops. Katie had been so excited about her history project that she'd totally forgotten about the track meet. "What's wrong? Was it canceled?" she asked Suzanne.

"No. Not for everyone. Just for us," Suzanne said angrily.

"What do you mean?"

"Coach Debbie is only letting the best runners compete. Andrew and Mandy are running in the relay race with two sixth-graders. Jeremy is running in one race and throwing a shot put. The rest of us fourth-graders are on the bench."

"That's not fair," Katie said. Her good mood was fading fast.

"I know," Suzanne agreed.

"There must be some mistake," Katie began.

Suzanne shook her head. "It's not a mistake. I saw it with my own eyes."

"We have to talk to Coach Debbie," Katie insisted.

"What for? She doesn't want to let us compete."

Katie took Suzanne by the hand and dragged her to the gym. "Come on," she insisted.

Coach Debbie was putting away basketballs when Katie and Suzanne walked into the gym. "Hi, girls," she greeted them. "Excited about our big meet on Thursday?"

"No," Suzanne answered.

"Uh, well, actually, that's what we're here to talk to you about," Katie said. "How come we're not running?"

"There are only a few races. I didn't have enough spaces for everyone," Coach Debbie explained.

"Jeremy's running *and* throwing the shot put," Suzanne told the coach. "Evan and Rachel from the fifth grade are running in two races. And that sixth-grader Maya is doing the long jump *and* the relay race."

"Well, *those* kids are really . . ." Coach Debbie began. Then she stopped herself. "Look, there are plenty of track meets this season. There's time for you to compete. For now, just think of yourselves as cheerleaders for the team."

Suzanne cocked her head to the side.

"Cheerleaders," she said. "Okay." A slow smile
formed on her face.

Katie looked at her friend strangely.
Suzanne had given in awfully quickly . . . for
her, anyway. There had to be a reason why.

So what was it?

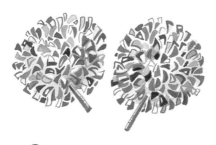

Chapter 9

"Okay, team, it's time to crush the competition!" Coach Debbie shouted as the track team gathered on the field. Of course, she was only talking to the few kids who were actually competing. She pretty much ignored the rest of them.

Suddenly, Suzanne raced onto the field.

"Wow!" Emma exclaimed, looking at Suzanne.

"What's she supposed to be?" a fifth-grader named Sophie asked.

Katie looked at her friend. Suzanne was wearing a bright red and white sweater and a short red skirt. And she was carrying red and white pom-poms. Suzanne was a cheerleader!

"Go, team! Go, team!" Suzanne shouted.

"Where did you find that uniform?" a sixth-grader named Lauren asked her.

"At the mall. It's red and white . . . our school colors."

"I didn't know we had school colors," George said.

"We do now," Suzanne told him. She shook her pom-poms right in his face.

Katie laughed. Now she knew why Suzanne had been so happy to be a cheerleader instead of a runner. She was getting more attention this way. Suzanne *loved* attention.

"We've got that spirit!" Suzanne cheered. "Come on, let's hear it."

But Coach Debbie wasn't thinking about

school spirit. She had only one thing on her mind. "We've got to WIN! WIN! WIN!" she shouted to the team. "Do whatever it takes. Just win!"

Katie was shocked. A teacher was supposed to tell the team to have fun and play fair. But Coach Debbie hadn't mentioned any of that.

Just then, the referee blew the whistle. It was time for the first race.

"That's me!" Jeremy told Katie.

"Good luck!" Katie said.

"Break a leg," Suzanne added.

Coach Debbie turned red in the face. "Why did you say that?" she demanded.

Suzanne gulped. "All I said was to break a leg. It's what actors say to wish each other luck."

"This *isn't* a theater," Coach Debbie reminded her. "It's a track meet. How can we WIN! WIN! WIN! if one of our best athletes has a broken leg?"

Suzanne looked like she was going to cry. "I'm sorry," she apologized.

"You should be," Coach Debbie said. Then she turned to Jeremy. "Get out there and pulverize the competition!"

× × ×

Jeremy did what Coach Debbie asked. He won, won, won his race!

"Wow!" Katie congratulated him. "You did it!"

"I was afraid not to. Coach Debbie would have been mad. Boy, is she scary!"

The two friends looked at their physical education teacher. She was jumping up and down beside the track.

"WIN! WIN! WIN!" Coach Debbie yelled as some sixth-graders ran a relay race. "You have to WIN! WIN! WIN!"

× × ×

Sure enough, Cherrydale Elementary School won their first track meet! It was very exciting. Especially when they all got to go out for ice cream.

"Next week, I want you guys to run even faster," Coach Debbie told the kids. "I want you to cause some major damage. Crush the competition. WIN! WIN! WIN!" She threw her hands up in the air. Her scoop of chocolate ice cream flew off the cone and landed on the ground with a splat! But Coach Debbie didn't seem to care.

George rolled his eyes. "She's going crazy," he whispered to Katie.

"Maybe it's because this was our first meet," Katie

replied. "I'm sure she'll be calmer next week."

"I hope so," George said. "I don't want to run if she's going to yell at me."

"We won't get to run," Kevin complained. "She's never going to give any of *us* a chance."

"Sure we will," Katie said. "Coach Debbie said there would be lots of chances for everyone to race. I'll bet anything that next week it will be our turn."

Chapter 10

When Coach Debbie posted a new list of runners for the next track meet, Katie's name wasn't there. Neither were Suzanne's, Emma's, George's, or Kevin's. The same kids who had run races last week were running again.

"This just isn't fair," George complained as he sat down on the grass next to Katie. "I don't know why I even came to this track meet."

"I could be spending my time working on my history project," Emma said. "I still have a lot of research to do."

"I'm quitting this team," Kevin said. "Who's with me?"

Katie thought about that for a moment. She and Kadeem still had work left to do on their project. But Kadeem had volunteered to do research by himself while Katie was at the track meet. He was really into it.

Still, Katie did sort of feel like she was wasting her time being at the track meet. But she wasn't a quitter.

"We can't quit," Katie said. "Not yet. It's only the second track meet. I'm sure things will get better. Maybe if we talk to Coach Debbie and ask her for a chance. She did promise Suzanne and me that . . ."

Katie didn't get to finish what she was saying. She was drowned out by Suzanne's cheering.

"Thunder, thunderation," she cheered. "We're the best team in the nation!"

Suzanne seemed really happy. It would be nice if Katie could have felt that way too. But Katie didn't really want to cheer. She wanted to run a race. Unfortunately, it didn't look like that was going to happen today.

Just then, Coach Debbie began to scream. "Oh, no! This is awful!" She stared at a note in her hand. "Maya has the flu! She's our best runner. We can't beat Apple Valley without her!"

"Can't someone else run her races?" Jeremy asked the coach.

Katie stood up and began jogging in place. She hoped Coach Debbie would see how much she wanted to WIN! WIN! WIN!

That was a great idea. Coach Debbie *did* notice her! "Katie," she called out. "I need you to run . . ."

"I'm ready!" Katie interrupted eagerly. "Which race?"

"Race?" Coach Debbie asked, confused. "Oh, no. I was going to ask you to run and get a bottle of cold water for *Evan*. He's going to compete in the long distance race Maya was supposed to run."

"But Evan is already running two races,"

Katie reminded the coach.

"I know," Coach Debbie replied. "That's why he needs more water. Now go, Katie. Hurry. The team is counting on you!"

Katie couldn't believe it! Now she was *really* mad. Coach Debbie was so mean! All she cared about was winning! She shouldn't be a teacher at all.

That was it! After today, Katie decided she was going to quit the team.

The gym was empty when Katie arrived. She hurried toward Coach Debbie's office, where the refrigerator was. Suddenly, she felt a cool breeze on the back of her neck.

Katie looked around. The nets on the basketball hoops weren't moving in the breeze. The papers on Coach Debbie's desk were completely still.

The breeze only seemed to be blowing around Katie.

Oh, no! This wasn't an ordinary wind. This

was the magic wind! It was back. And there was nothing Katie could do to stop it!

Whoosh! The magic wind picked up speed. It swirled wildly around Katie. It was powerful and out of control. Katie was really scared.

But she was even more scared when the wind *stopped* blowing. She knew what that meant. The magic wind was gone . . .

And so was Katie Carew.

Chapter 11

Katie opened her eyes slowly and looked around. Wow! That had been some strong wind. It had blown Katie right out of the gym. Now she was standing in the middle of the track field.

Okay, so now she knew *where* she was. But she still didn't know *who* she was.

"Coach Debbie!" she heard Evan shout. "Do you want me to run this race for Maya?"

There was no answer. Katie looked around for the coach. She didn't see her anywhere.

"Do you want me to run now?" Evan asked again. Then he gave Katie a funny look. "Are you okay, *Coach Debbie*?"

Katie gulped. Evan had been talking to *her*! Slowly, she looked down at her body. Katie wasn't wearing her lucky cocker spaniel T-shirt anymore. Instead, she was wearing a shirt that said "Winners Never Quit." She had a silver whistle hanging around her neck. And her own red sneakers had been replaced with a pair of very white, very large running shoes.

Coach Debbie's running shoes!

Oh, no! Katie had turned into Coach Debbie. Right in the middle of the big meet! This was *so* not good.

Or was it . . . ?

Just then, Katie got another one of her great ideas. "No, Evan," she told him. "I think you've run enough. It's time to give someone else a chance." She turned to Kevin. "You run in this race."

"Huh?" Kevin asked.

"I said, 'Run this race,' " Katie repeated. She tried to sound strict. Just like the real Coach Debbie.

Kevin was shocked. But he wasn't going to give up his chance to run. "Okay!" he shouted excitedly as he ran for the starting line.

As soon as the referee said, "Go!" Kevin took off like a shot. He ran the fastest he ever had.

"Suzanne, go cheer for him," Katie told her best friend. "Show him we have spirit. *Lots of spirit*!"

"Sure, Coach!" Suzanne agreed. She leaped up and ran toward the track.

"Let's go, Kevin!" she cheered as she waved her pom-poms wildly.

Katie grinned. Things were going great . . . until Suzanne threw her pom-poms high in the air. She managed to catch one of them. But the other pom-pom flew off in the direction of the track. It landed right on Kevin's head! He couldn't see.

Kevin got all turned around. *He started running in the wrong direction!*

"No, Kevin!" Katie shouted. "That way!"

Kevin stopped, whipped the pom-pom from his face, and spun around. But it was too late. He'd lost the race.

"Suzanne! What did you do?" one of the sixth-grade boys shouted.

"I can't believe you made him lose!" a fifth-grade girl added.

Suzanne looked like she was going to cry. This wasn't the attention she wanted from the older kids. "Coach Debbie told me to cheer!" she swore to them. "It's all her fault."

Katie frowned. It was the truth. She *had* been the one to tell Suzanne to cheer. What a mistake that had been.

But there was nothing Katie could do about it now.

"Look, you guys," she said finally. "It's just one race. Besides, winning isn't everything."

The kids stared at her in amazement.

"Coach Debbie, are you sick or something?" Rachel asked her.

Katie shook her head. "Sure, winning is great. But so is teamwork, and fun! *That's* what this team should be about."

She looked at her clipboard. "Okay, the next race is the hurdles. Suzanne, you're perfect for this."

Suzanne gulped. "Me?" she asked nervously. "But I've never jumped over a real hurdle before."

"You can do it. You've got long, strong legs. Like a racehorse."

Suzanne gave Katie a look. Katie knew that Suzanne probably didn't like being compared to an animal. But she also knew that she wasn't going to argue with her coach. Not when she was actually giving her a chance to run.

"Okay." Suzanne started to run toward the track.

"Uh, Suzanne?" Katie stopped her.

"Yes?"

"Leave the pom-poms back here."

Suzanne dropped her pom-poms and hurried off to the starting line.

As soon as the referee blew his whistle, Suzanne ran as fast as she could to the first hurdle. She cleared it easily.

Suzanne was doing really well! Katie was so happy. If Suzanne won this race, the kids would forget about what had happened with Kevin and the pom-poms.

More importantly, it would prove that other kids could WIN! WIN! WIN! too.

Suzanne took the next hurdle just as easily. But the third one was much higher. Suzanne had never jumped over anything that tall. She leaped up into the air, and . . .

"Ouch!" she cried out as her knee hit the wooden hurdle. Suzanne flipped over onto the ground. Her skirt flew up in the air. Good thing she was wearing shorts under her skirt! Otherwise everyone would have seen her underpants. How embarrassing would that have been? It was bad enough that she'd lost the race!

"Hey, Coach," Evan said as Suzanne walked back over toward the team. "Next time you want to put that horse in for a race, I vote *neigh*!"

Suzanne looked like she was about to cry.

Chapter 12

Unfortunately, Katie couldn't take the time to make her best friend feel better just then. There was still one more race to run.

"The next race is the relay," Katie told her team. "Emma, you're going to take the first lap."

Emma seemed a little surprised. So did the rest of the kids.

Next, Katie turned to Annabelle, a tall, thin fifth-grader who was a fast runner. She could help the team if Emma fell behind. "Annabelle, you take lap number two. Rachel, you're third. Mike, you take fourth, and . . ."

Katie looked around for a minute, trying

to find just the right person to finish the relay. "And for the final lap, how about . . ." She took a deep breath. *"George."*

Everyone gasped. *Especially George.* "Not me, Coach! I'm always last!"

"You're getting better every day," Katie reminded him. "I have faith in you."

"I wish *I* did," George said. He looked at his teammates. "I'm sorry . . . in advance."

$$\times \quad \times \quad \times$$

"On your marks. Get set. Go!"

As soon as the referee blew his whistle, Emma ran as fast as she could down the track. Katie had never seen her friend's legs move so quickly.

"Go, Emma!" Katie shouted excitedly. "You can do it. Try your best!"

The kids all stared at her.

"What happened to 'Win! Win! Win!'?" Rachel asked Kevin.

Emma kept up the pace. But the first Apple Valley relay runner was quick. She

pulled ahead of Emma early on, and never
lost the lead. By the time Emma passed the
relay baton to Annabelle, Apple Valley was
way ahead.

Luckily, Annabelle was a super speedy
runner. She soon caught up to the Apple
Valley runner. They were practically tied
as they came around the bend.

Katie's heart began to pound. Rachel
would be next, and then Mike. They were
both really fast runners. It looked like
Cherrydale Elementary had a chance to win
the relay!

Then Katie remembered something: *George
was the last runner in the relay.*

Suddenly, it didn't seem like such a great
idea to have George run. He was probably
going to lose his part of the race. And if he
did, Apple Valley Elementary would have
enough points to win the whole track meet.

"I can't look," Katie groaned.

As Annabelle handed her baton to Rachel,

Katie turned and ran off to hide behind a thick tree at the other end of the field. Katie couldn't see a thing. The track team couldn't see her either.

In the distance, she heard kids cheering loudly. Katie hoped it was her team cheering. Suddenly, she felt like she really *was* Coach Debbie. She wanted to win that badly.

But the real Coach Debbie would have pulled George out of the race. And Katie would never *ever* do that.

Suddenly, a fiercely cold wind began to blow. Katie pulled Coach Debbie's sweat jacket tight around her. The leaves on the trees were still. The grass wasn't moving either. Katie knew right away that this was no ordinary wind. This was the magic wind!

The magic wind grew stronger and stronger. It whirled around Katie like a tornado. Faster and faster it blew, until the wind was so strong, Katie could barely breathe.

And then it stopped. Just like that. The magic wind was gone.

Katie Kazoo was back!

Of course, that also meant that Coach Debbie was back too. And Katie had a feeling she wasn't going to be too happy to see George in the race.

Chapter 13

"George, what are you doing? Get back here!" Coach Debbie shouted as she ran over to the starting line.

"But you told me to run this race," George told her.

"I did not . . ." Coach Debbie said angrily. She stopped for a minute. She was very confused. "I mean . . . I would never put you . . . at least I don't think . . ."

"You said he could run the last lap. We all heard you," Kevin insisted.

Coach Debbie frowned. "But . . . I . . . wouldn't . . . would I? Oh, I don't know what I did." She seemed confused. But only for a moment. "However, I *do* know this," she said firmly. "I'm pulling you out now!"

"You can't do that," the referee told Coach Debbie. "Once he's standing by the starting line, he has to run the race. It's the rule."

"Oh, no. We've lost this one," Coach Debbie moaned.

George frowned. He felt terrible.

Katie felt badly too. All she'd wanted to do was give her friend a chance to run. But George wasn't ready for such a big challenge.

And now everyone was going to be mad at him for losing.

Katie looked out at the track. Mike had just started to run his lap. He was way in the lead. Cherrydale could have a chance—if George could pull it together enough to win his lap.

Suddenly, Katie had another one of her great ideas. Sure, George wasn't as fast as the Apple Valley runner. But he had something the other kid didn't.

She ran over to the starting line. "George!" she shouted.

"Go away," George said sadly.

"No. Listen. Here's what you gotta do," she said. "Make him laugh."

"What?"

"Make him laugh," Katie repeated. "He can't run fast if he's laughing."

George's eyes lit up. "Hey, that's right!" he said excitedly.

As soon as George grabbed the baton from Mike, he took off down the track. But he didn't run like the other kids did. Instead, George made his legs wobble and wiggle. He twirled around like a ballerina. Then he leaped up in the air and did a goofy clown-like split.

"Check him out!" an Apple Valley kid said.

"He's so funny!" another agreed.

Everyone was laughing at George. Sam, the boy running for the Apple Valley team, turned around to see what was happening. He began to chuckle too. He couldn't help it.

"That's it, George!" Katie shouted to him. "It's working! Now run!"

George ran as fast as he could. He actually caught up with Sam!

"Tell him a joke!" Katie yelled to George.

"You know who the best runner in history was?" George asked between huffs and puffs.

Sam couldn't believe George was asking him questions in the middle of a race. He stared at him in amazement.

"Adam," George joked. "He was first in the *human* race!"

Sam started to laugh again.

Now George began to run faster than he ever had before. As he pulled ahead of Sam, he left him with one last joke. "You know how fireflies start a race? On your marks! Get set! Glow!"

Sam giggled so hard that he had to bend over and hold his belly. That left the track wide open for George. A few moments later, he crossed the finish line way ahead of Sam.

George had led Cherrydale Elementary School to victory!

The Apple Valley coach stormed over to Coach Debbie. "Your team cheated," he shouted at her. "That kid made my runner laugh."

Coach Debbie shrugged. "I don't see anything in the rule book against that. Can I help it if your runner can't concentrate on the race?" Coach Debbie answered. "My team WON! WON! WON!"

The Apple Valley coach looked angry. But Coach Debbie was right. George had been sneaky. But he hadn't cheated.

As the other coach stormed off, Coach Debbie looked at George. "Well, you did it," she told him.

"Thanks for putting me in, Coach," George grinned. "That was fun."

"It's not about f . . ." Coach Debbie began. Then she thought about it. "I guess it *is* about fun," she admitted. "And that was very clever of you."

"Thanks," George said, taking a bow. "But it was all Katie's idea."

"Well, it isn't going to happen again," the coach continued.

"That's not fair!" Katie shouted out. "Even kids who aren't the fastest runners should be allowed to try."

Coach Debbie nodded. "I agree. I didn't say George wasn't going to run any more races."

"What do you mean?" George asked her.

"I'll put you in again, but you'll have to win on your sports ability. Not your jokes."

George frowned. "I don't have a chance."

"Sure you do," Coach Debbie assured him. "There are other competitions besides relay races at a track meet. I liked that split you did in the air. With a little work, you could be a top-notch hurdle jumper."

Suzanne frowned. That was definitely not *her* talent.

"I'm not sure what happened here today," Coach Debbie continued, "but George reminded me of something I'd forgotten a long time ago. The best way to win at anything is with teamwork. You guys have different talents. We need to use them all."

George leaped in the air and spun around like a crazy ballerina. "I'm ready!" he teased.

Chapter 14

"Okay, Kadeem, this is it," Katie announced on Monday morning. They were standing out in the hall, waiting to go into the classroom and do their history presentation.

"It's all under control," Kadeem assured her.

Katie smiled. Kadeem had turned out to be a pretty cool partner. He was smart, and really creative too. In fact, the costumes for their presentation had been his idea. They were really wild.

Katie was wearing a big box around her body. On her head, she wore a hat with a hanger glued to it. That was supposed to be her old-fashioned TV antennae.

As Katie walked into the classroom, the kids all pointed at her and laughed. But she didn't care. That was the whole point of dressing like a TV set!

"Our report is on the history of TV comedies," Katie told the class. "We watched lots of old videos to see what the first TV shows were like. We found out that the first big TV star was a funny guy named Milton Berle. People called him Uncle Miltie." She turned toward the door.

Kadeem entered the room. He was wearing a dress!

"Check out Kadeem!" Andrew giggled.

Kadeem curtsied low. He fell over onto the floor.

The kids laughed.

"Uncle Miltie wore goofy dresses and hats on his TV show, to make people laugh," Kadeem told everyone. "He was especially good at a kind of comedy called slapstick.

That's when the actor falls down, bangs his head, or does other silly things just for a laugh."

"I think his *face* is good for a laugh," Katie told the class. "Don't you?"

The kids all stared at her. They couldn't believe she was saying something so mean, right in the middle of her history presentation!

Kadeem walked to the corner of the room and picked up a huge whipped-cream pie. He and Katie had hidden it there earlier.

"You wouldn't dare," Katie said, staring at the pie.

Kadeem winked at the class.

Bam! Kadeem smashed the pie . . . *right in his own face.*

The kids in the class laughed really, really hard. They hadn't expected that!

"That's the kind of comedy people watched on old-fashioned TV shows," Kadeem explained as he licked the cream from his chin.

Katie laughed along with everyone else.

Kadeem was hysterical. She was so lucky to have the two funniest kids in the fourth grade in her class.

Suddenly, Katie felt something cold and wet hit her right on the nose. It felt like a gooey kind of rain. She looked around the classroom. It didn't seem to be raining on anybody else.

Oh, no! Had the magic wind returned? Was it bringing rain or hail with it now? Was it going to change her into someone else, right here, in front of her whole class?

Some of the wet stuff dripped into Katie's mouth. *Yum!* It hadn't been the magic wind at all. It was whipped cream. Kadeem had thrown a handful of it at her when she wasn't looking.

Katie was really glad she was going to be herself for a while. Especially when there was pie around. "Mmm . . ." Katie giggled as she scraped some pie off her cheek and tasted it. "Banana cream. My favorite!"

Spice up Your Sneakers

George and Suzanne were really proud of their new sneakers. But Katie and Jeremy had been wearing the same old sneaks for a long time. Their running shoes had started to look run-down. Luckily, they knew exactly how to fancy up their footwear. Now you can too!

Just be sure to get your parents' permission before you start.

You will need:

A pencil	Newspaper
Glitter	Your sneakers (of course!)
Fabric paints	

Here's what you do:

Spread the newspaper out on a table. Use the pencil to draw a design on your sneakers. Here are some ideas:

- ✳ A shooting star like the one Katie wished on.

- ✳ A soccer ball—that's Jeremy's favorite design.

- ✳ Lightning bolts to show just how fast you can run!

Use the fabric paint to color in your drawing. Just remember, fabric paint is permanent. Once it's on your sneaker, it's there for good.

If, like Suzanne, you want to add some sparkle to your sneaks, try mixing some glitter into your fabric paint before you use it.

Okay! Ready? On your mark, get set, PAINT!